Ruby and the Booker Boys

Ruby Flips for Attention

Other *RUBY* books
by Derrick Barnes

Brand-new School, Brave New Ruby
Trivia Queen, 3rd Grade Supreme
The Slumber Party Payback

Ruby and the Booker Boys

Ruby Flips for Attention

by **Derrick Barnes**

illustrated by **Vanessa Brantley Newton**

SCHOLASTIC INC.

New York   Toronto   London   Auckland   Sydney
Mexico City   New Delhi   Hong Kong   Buenos Aires

No part of this publication may be reproduced, stored in a retrieval system, or transmitted in any form or by any means, electronic, mechanical, photocopying, recording, or otherwise, without written permission of the publisher. For information regarding permission, write to Scholastic Inc., Attention: Permissions Department, 557 Broadway, New York, NY 10012.

ISBN-13: 978-0-545-01763-3   ISBN-10: 0-545-01763-7

Text copyright © 2009 by Derrick Barnes
Illustrations copyright © 2009 by Scholastic Inc.

All rights reserved. Published by Scholastic Inc.

SCHOLASTIC, LITTLE APPLE, and associated logos are trademarks and/or registered trademarks of Scholastic Inc.

Library of Congress Cataloging-in-Publication Data Available

12 11 10 9 8 7 6 5 4 3   10 11 12 13 14/0

Printed in the U.S.A.   40
First printing, April 2009

To the students at Pershing East in Chicago.

Thanks, Mrs. Hill.

Sylvia Watley – thanks for giving me a shot.
I've come a long way since Hershey Brown.
– D.B.

☆ Chapters ☆

Here's the deal: Daddy and Ma took me to see my teenage cousin Kee-Kee and her drill team, the Wallace Park Spirit. Seeing those amazing flips and perfect steps makes me want to start my own squad. We'll dance better and flip higher. I can't wait to dance and flip and hear the crowd scream *my* name. Watch out, Cousin Kee-Kee — here comes Ruby!

— rb

❋★❋★1❋★❋★
Kee-Kee

"Those are our seats. Right there! Right there!" I yelled, and pointed after I zoomed through the big red gym doors.

Ma called out to me, "Slow down, baby. You're going to run somebody over. Those seats aren't going anywhere." I was running to the bleachers before somebody took *our* seats. Daddy bought tickets for all of us. There was one for me, two for my parents, and a ticket for one of my big brothers, Tyner.

I had never been to a real drill team show before. We came to cheer on my cousin Keeva, who I call Kee-Kee. She's fifteen years old and the captain of her squad, the Wallace Park Spirit. Kee-Kee's super-extra-pretty, and she's got style. And also, she's a very good flipper. Ma says Kee-Kee's talent runs in the family.

"Hold on, sweetness," Daddy called out to me. "The show won't start for another ten minutes."

"I know, Daddy. I just want to make sure we can see. We do have a good view, right, Daddy?" I asked. The last time Daddy took us to a show, I couldn't even see the stage.

"We've got a great view, Ruby, you'll see," Daddy said. He had his arm around Ma. He grabbed my hand and led us to our seats.

Ty dragged real slowly behind us. His chubby cheeks looked droopy. He wasn't too excited to be at the drill team show. "Ma, can I walk home now?"

"Come on, Ty. Don't be like that, baby. It's too far to walk home." Ma turned around and snagged Ty's hand. "Keeva is going to be so happy to see all of us in the crowd. Let's show her some love."

"Okay," Ty moaned. It's not like he was really going to leave. It was getting dark outside, plus the walk from Eastview High School to our house is a long one. The only reason he came is because Kee-Kee came to his last science fair. She cheered and screamed for that boy and his solar-powered popcorn popper like he was a rock star. I guess he felt he owed her one. Ty is just that kind of boy. I like that about him.

Ro and Marcellus, my *older* big brothers, said that there was no way they'd sit through one minute of "flips and pom-poms."

Daddy had dropped them off at the

home of his best friend, Melvin. We call Melvin Uncle Too Cool. Uncle Too Cool has two sons who are around Marcellus's age. They were probably having fun doing the stupid stuff boys do.

The gym was packed like there was going to be a big championship basketball game. There was a DJ blaring hip-hop from his speakers. The drumbeats bounced off the shiny hardwood floors. The bottoms of sneakers squeaked like tickled mice as people piled into the bleachers.

"Here, hold my hand, Ty. I don't want you to get lost," I told my brother.

Ty may be older than me, but he doesn't like to be in big groups.

Daddy got to our seats. He bowed like a true gentleman to Ma and me, and held out his hand. "Ladies, you first." My daddy is so nice.

Ma gave Daddy one of her pretty smiles that I like so much. She said, "Why, thank you, sir, so very much."

They laughed as Daddy kissed her on the cheek. I think it's cute when he does that.

As soon as we were about to take our seats, I spotted Kee-Kee's mom. Her name is Zenny, but we all call her Aunt Z. She waved for us to come closer to her seats. "Hey! Over here! Over here!" Aunt Z is pretty just like Ma. They almost look like twins, except Ma's skin is the color of *smooooth* peanut butter, and Aunt Z has skin like a cup of hot cocoa.

"Hey, Z! I know you're excited, girl." Ma grinned and giggled before she hugged her sister tight. Then Ma pulled away and said, with her hands on her hips, "So, why didn't you call me back last night? You knew I had some juicy news to tell you —"

"Um," Daddy interrupted quickly. He knew that if he didn't say hello to Aunt Z, they'd get lost in their sister talk. He gave her a big hug, too, and then asked, "Where's Blue, Z?" Uncle Blue is Aunt Z's husband. He's a short little man, but his heart is as big as a dinosaur egg. He's one of the nicest men I know — second only to my daddy.

"Honey, he had to go back out to the car to get his glasses. That man is always forgetting something. I don't know what he'd do without me." Aunt Z laughed. Then she gave me a hug and left me covered with her sweet, fancy-smelling perfume. "Hey, Miss Ruby. How's it going?"

"It's going good, Aunt Z. I just can't wait until the show starts," I told her.

Our row of seats was very crowded. Ty stood in the way of a *big-big-big* man and kept him from returning to his seat. The man looked like a grizzly bear wearing jeans and a sweater. He was holding a big stack of snacks in his arms. It seemed like he couldn't wait to gobble that stuff up. He looked

annoyed at Ty. Ty didn't notice the man. He was too busy pushing his glasses up on his nose.

"Daddy, you know what would be so great right now? Snacks, Daddy. Snacks!" Ty was talking like he'd never had a snack before in his life. "You know — popcorn, hot dogs, and nachos. I *love* nachos, Daddy," Ty was begging.

"Sure, son." Daddy grinned and handed Ty a twenty-dollar bill. "Get what you want."

Aunt Z folded her arms and gave Ty that look that says, "Oh, no, you didn't," and then she told him, "Boy, you better bring your cute little self over here and give your auntie a kiss." Ty gave Aunt Z a lightning-quick hug and a teeny-tiny kiss. He wasn't going to let Aunt Z hold up his quest for nachos. No way.

He turned to me and asked, "Hey, Rube, you want something? Wanna come with me? I'll split it with you." Ty and I are official, unofficial best friends. He's so sweet to me.

"Ty, you know what I haven't had in a *long* time? Strawberry licorice. Let's go get some!" I grabbed Ty's hand and pulled him toward the snack stand.

"Bring me an orange soda, baby," Ma told Ty.

Daddy put in his order. "Peanuts for me, big guy."

*　*　*

When we left the snack stand, Ty was all smiles. He had Ma's orange soda, peanuts for Daddy, my strawberry licorice, one jumbo tub of extra-cheesy nachos with *holler-peen-yo* peppers, and a large grape soda with extra ice. He could barely see over everything he was carrying.

"Need some help, Ty?" I giggled while chewing on my licorice.

"No, Rube, I got it."

"I don't want you to spill those nachos. You'll have a fit," I said to Ty as we stood in the mouth of the tunnel that led to our seats.

That's when Ty accidentally dropped Daddy's peanuts. When we both bent down to pick them up, the big lights in the gym went dim. The DJ got on the microphone and introduced Cousin Kee-Kee and her squad.

"Welcome to the Eastview High Drill Team Competition! Our first contestants are last month's champions.

Stand and give a warm round of applause to the one and only Wallace Park Spirit!!!"

I snatched up the peanuts and left Ty behind. Zooming through the tunnel, I could hear the *SWOOSH* and feel the *SWIRL* of the excitement in my ears. When I made it back inside, there were Kcc-Kee and the other Wallace Park Spirit members.

The entire squad had on the cutest red-white-and-gold uniforms that a cheer team could wear. The girls had sparkles on their skirts and pom-poms on their sneakers. The boys had on red-and-gold tank tops.

Kee-Kee was in front of the whole team. She was in total control. The thump of the music sounded like the heartbeats of a million elephants. Everyone rose to their feet as the Wallace Park Spirit amazed us with their dance routines, cartwheels, and backflips.

"Rube? Hey, Rube? Is anybody home?" Ty had found his way to me from the tunnel. He seemed shaken up. "Hey, girl, don't leave me like that." Ty waved his hand in front of my face. I was in a trance. I plunked down in the first empty seat I saw. Daddy's peanuts fell to the floor again.

Kee-Kee was doing flips that I didn't even know she could do. It was the most awesome thing I'd ever seen! At the end of the show, one of the big boys on the team lifted Kee-Kee into the air. Kee-Kee was so high up, I thought she would get stuck in the ceiling or go through it. But instead, she landed at the top of a big pyramid that the other boy members had formed. She stood out like the star on top of a Christmas tree.

"That's my baby, everybody! That's my baby!" Aunt Z clapped and yelled loud enough to be heard all over.

The music stopped booming, the Wallace Park Spirit stood still, and then the crowd cheered like crazy. A huge crowd of teenagers started to chant: *"Kee-Kee! Kee-Kee! Kee-Kee!"*

Then — it hit me. I knew what I had to do. This would be just the thing that could bring me the popularity that my brothers steal from me every single day. I had to start my very own super-fantastic drill team! I could see it in my

head. I was going to be the one standing on top of a pyramid while everyone cheered and chanted *my* name: *"Ruby! Ruby! Ruby!"*

Right in the middle of my grand plans to take Cousin Kee-Kee's spot as the drill team princess, Ty tapped me on my shoulder and knocked me out of my dream world. "There's a peanut by your feet. We need to get back to our seats, Rube."

I didn't even answer him. The only thing on my mind was getting started on the best flipping and dancing drill team in Bellow Rock.

2

The Chill Brook Steppers

"**O**kay, ladies, listen up!" I paced back and forth on the sidewalk in front of our stoop. "You all know why you're here, and I hope you mean business."

My girl Teresa Petticoat and I had made up flyers for my new drill team: the Chill Brook Steppers. I came up with the name myself. The thing was, you had to live on Chill Brook Avenue to be in the squad.

We had hopped on our bikes and taped up flyers from Fifty-fourth to

Sixtieth Streets. But only three girls showed up — Toya Tribbles and the Piccolo twins, Peaches and Plenty. That was okay. It was really five counting Teresa and me. I bet Kee-Kee's squad, the Wallace Park Spirit, started out small, too.

"So tell me something, girlie, when do we get our *fancy* outfits like yours?" Teresa asked. "I love that red-and-pink sparkly getup you're sporting."

"Yeah, Ruby Booker. Are you the only one who gets to be cute?" Toya Tribbles wondered. She was the only fifth-grader who showed up. I was happy that she made it. She's popular at our school, Hope Road Academy. I knew that if she joined the Chill Brook Steppers, we'd really be something.

"Well, first of all, I'm the only member so far," I told Toya and the rest of the girls. The truth was, Ma only had enough material to make a uniform for me the night before. Plus, I didn't know how many girls would show up to join the drill team.

"So what do we have to . . ." Peaches Piccolo started to say.

". . . do to make the team, Ruby?" Plenty Piccolo finished up. That's how they talk. Peaches starts a sentence and Plenty finishes it up.

I can hardly tell the Piccolo twins

apart. They both have pretty hair and big eyes. When Plenty laughs, I can tell the difference between her and Peaches. Plenty's laugh sounds like she has a squeaky rubber ducky in her nose. The Piccolos are a strange set of girls, but they're so fun to have around.

"For starters, we're going to look cute, as you can see." I twirled around and modeled my outfit.

"Yeah, yeah, we get all of that, but if we're the Steppers, when do we get to step?" Toya asked.

"Besides being the cutest drill team in Bellow Rock, we're going to be the highest flying squad, too," I promised

them. "We'll perform cartwheels and triple-double backflips and stuff like that."

Teresa looked worried. "Who's gonna do the flipping, Ruby? You didn't say a thing about us *flipping*."

"Didn't I? It must have slipped my mind," I said.

Teresa asked, "Who's going to teach us all of that stuff, Ruby? You don't know a thing about cartwheels or handstands or flips, girlie." Teresa was right, but I wish she hadn't said that in front of the twins and Toya.

"Now, T, I may not know how to flip, but with the music playing and the lights down low during our shows, no one is even going to pay attention," I told her. "People will be more interested in watching us at the beginning of each show when we strut out in our skirts and look like the best drill team in Bellow Rock."

Peaches had a puzzled look on her face. "Are you . . ." she began.

". . . serious, Ruby Booker?" Plenty finished the question.

"Yes, I'm *serious*. Can't you just hear the crowd screaming our names?" I held a hand up to my ear, closed my eyes, and just imagined how roaring loud our fans would cheer.

Toya was starting to question my grand ideas. "How about dancing? Are we going to pretend like we can dance, too?" Her attitude was showing, and it wasn't pretty.

I didn't know what to say to that. "I guess we will . . . well, we could dance a little. . . ." My ma is a perfect dancer and an even better dance teacher, but I can't dance at all. I don't know how that happened, but it's true. I was born with no dance talent.

Teresa came in closer to me and whispered, "What will we do now? You dance like a crazed chickadee."

That made me admit it to everyone. "I can't dance too well, but Peaches and Plenty, I know you two can. And you, too, Toya," I said.

Peaches and Plenty showed off some dance moves. Peaches said, "There aren't any other twins who can . . ."

". . . tear up a dance floor like the Piccolos," Plenty added.

Toya began to question my drill team leadership. "So let me get this straight, Ruby. You can't do flips?"

"Uh, not really," I answered.

"You can't dance, either?" Toya was starting to get on my nerves.

"Nope. But I could probably learn some easy stepping moves, maybe," I said.

"Great," Toya said. "Instead of coming here, I could have gone shopping downtown with my big sister." Toya was really angry. She balled up one of the flyers and tossed it at me. I caught it. Then she rolled her eyes and started to walk back up Chill Brook Avenue toward her house. But before she left, she looked at me and said, "Girl, when you've got more than that cute little red-and-pink outfit to show me, give me a call."

Teresa tried to get Toya to stay. "Don't go, Toya. I'm sure Ruby's got something else up her sleeves. You *do* have something up your sleeves, don't you, Ruby?" Teresa asked me.

I just rolled up one of the sleeves to show her that I really didn't have anything else up my sleeves at that time. I hunched my shoulders and sat down on the bottom step of my stoop.

Peaches looped her sister by the arm and said, "Same here, Ruby. We're . . ."

". . . out of here." Plenty and Peaches went the opposite direction of Toya, arm in arm, down Chill Brook Avenue.

So there we were. Teresa and I were the pitiful only members of the Chill Brook Steppers.

Teresa took a seat right next to me on the stoop. "It's just you and me, T." I put my arm around her. "I guess we can call ourselves the Chill Brook Two-Steppers."

Teresa laughed and laughed. "You

are so crazy, Ruby Booker. I guess
you're right. I know one thing."

"What's that, T?" I asked.

"We need some help, badly."

Teresa was right. But who could
teach me how to dance and flip in a
day or two?

✿★✿★3✿★✿★

Help a Sister Out

"**G**irl, are you crazy?" Ro laughed. I had asked him to teach me how to do backflips. I would have asked Marcellus first, but I bumped into Ro's bigheaded self when he was on his way out the door.

"Come on, Ro. I promise not to get on your nerves for a week," I begged.

"You know how many times I've heard that? Besides, I've got to go down to The Booker Box to defend my gaming crown. Who plays *All-Star Football* better than me?" he asked.

"Nobody, Ro. Nobody," I agreed with my lips turned up. Ro thinks he's all that, but he's not. Other than coming up with new prank ideas, beating kids at his favorite video games is his favorite thing to do.

"You've got it, shorty. See you later." Ro grabbed his backpack, then headed out the door in a flash.

* * *

Even though Ro said no, I knew Ty would help me, right? Wrong. I changed my clothes and ran down to his room, knocked lightly, and said real sweetly, *"Tyyyyner, it's Ruuuuby."*

When I asked Ty to help me, he said, "No way, Rube. I won't be the cause of

you breaking every bone in your body. Count me out." Ty wouldn't even look at me. He sat at his desk organizing my math flash cards so he could help me study.

"Come on, Ty. How can I be the leader of a super-ultra-awesome cheer squad if *I* can't even do a flip?"

"I just don't want you to get hurt, that's all," Ty said. "Ask Marcellus."

"He's always so busy," I said with my arms folded.

"You'll never know until you ask," Ty said.

"Where's Marcellus now?" I asked.

"He's out in the backyard, fixing

the wheels on his bike." Ty pointed to the door.

I zoomed outside. Marcellus was my last hope.

When I got out back, Marcellus was adding red wheels to his black-and-silver bike. As soon as I asked, Marcellus said, "Sure. I'll help you, ladybug."

Ty was right. Marcellus, or, as he's called, "Big-Time," is good at almost

everything: school, drumming, music, basketball, spelling big words, you name it. He's even an awesome flipper, too. And he never lets me down.

"Will you? I mean, thanks, Marcellus. I knew you would help me, and that's great!" I said, really fast and excited. Marcellus is a seventh-grader at our school. Everybody looks up to him, even some eighth-graders.

"Okay, okay, calm down. I just hate to see you all bummed out. You think I'd pass up a chance to help out my little sis flip and fly in the air? If you want to learn the right way, I'm the kid to see, right?" Marcellus had a big grin on his face.

"You're the kid!" I answered.

"Everybody should call me Do-It-All, because there's nothing I can't do." Marcellus went on and on talking so big about himself. Typical Marcellus, but I love him. "I mean, I've never taught anyone how to flip before, but I figure that since I'm good at it, I should be able to teach it."

We shook hands like Daddy does when he greets people at The Booker Box. I guess this time I was kind of like the customer for Marcellus. I just hoped I'd get what I'd bargained for.

4
Bend It Like Booker

Marcellus and I headed down to the basement. I even brought my pet, Lady Love. I'm probably the only eight-year-old girl in the world with a pet iguana. She sat on an old foot cushion and watched my first flip lesson.

I couldn't believe that Marcellus "Big-Time" Booker was helping me. He even cleared out all of the boxes, Ty's good-grade trophies, and a lot of other brainy cool stuff so that we'd have enough space. Carefully, he slid

his drums to the side.
If he even scratched
a drumstick, he would
just lose his mind. He
then rolled up the
long carpet to get it
out of the way.

"I've seen this a million times on TV, ladybug. Trust me. You're going to do just fine. But you've got to listen to everything I tell you so that you don't get hurt," Marcellus said, sounding just like Coach Tuma, our gym teacher at school.

"Yeah, yeah, yeah," I said, rushing

him. "So when do we get to the super-double flips and stuff?" I asked Marcellus. I couldn't wait to get my "Kee-Kee" on.

"First we have to warm up and stretch, ladybug. You can't just get to it. Then we'll try a couple of cartwheels," Marcellus said as he held both of my hands. "Hey, Kee-Kee was once little just like you. She had to start somewhere. One step at a time, baby sis, and I know that you can be just as good as Kee-Kee."

I looked him up and down like he was crazy and said, "Cartwheels? That's baby stuff, Marcellus."

"Come on, girl. Do you want me to help you or not? If you just listen to me, you'll be doing flips within a month or so. I just know it." Marcellus tried to treat me like a real little kid, but I wasn't hearing it. I didn't have time to waste.

"Whatever you say, Marcellus," I told him, but I wasn't really listening. I was going to do my own thing. I just needed him to get me started, that was all.

"Look, if you don't want me to coach you, that's cool. I guess you're comfortable just being a fan of the number one drill team in Wallace Park.

I'll go back to what I was doing," Marcellus said before he started to walk back up the stairs. I grabbed his arm.

"Okay! Okay! Let's go . . . right now!" I ordered.

"That's the Ruby I know!" Marcellus said. Lady Love made her little *click-hiss* kind of sound. She does that when she doesn't like something. I don't think she liked the idea of me flipping. Maybe she was right.

We sat on the floor and touched our tippy-toes with our fingers. We stood up and bent our backs in an L shape. Then we held our arms straight out and twisted around like two helicopters. I was so bored. None of that stuff had anything to do with flipping!

"Okay . . . now what?" I asked. That was enough stretching.

"Well, it's easy. Just go back a few feet and face me," Marcellus coached. I followed his instructions and stood there, waiting on his next step.

I took my shoes off and bounced up and down. I was starting to feel it . . . whatever "it" was. "Come on, Coach. I'm pumped up. Let's do this!" I balled up my fist and pounded it in my other hand. That's what Ro does when he gets excited about something. It stung a little bit, but I can get tough, too . . . I *can*.

"Now, all you have to do is run as fast as you can toward me. Right before you reach me, do a tiny cartwheel. That's it. I want to see how easy that is for you. We're taking it slow, remember?" Marcellus asked.

"Uh . . . yeah. Sure. Taking it slow. I got it." There was no way I was taking it slow. All I kept thinking about was how easy Kee-Kee made it look. If she could do it, then so could I.

"You can do it. Trust me," Marcellus said as he looked at me and nodded his head.

I just stood there for about ten seconds, thinking. I had Marcellus fooled. He thought I was going to run all the way toward him and do a weak little cartwheel. Not me. I was going to try that big backflip that I saw Kee-Kee do.

Suddenly, I decided to just take off running. I saw Kee-Kee in my mind again. She had looked so pretty that night. I heard the crowd in my ears cheering her on, and then they started cheering my name: *"Ruby! Ruby! Ruby!"*

Halfway to Marcellus, I could see him smiling. I closed my eyes for a second and thought, *Here goes nothing.*

"Come on. You got it!" Marcellus yelled in support.

I slowed down a little, did a cartwheel, and then my left foot landed kind of twisted. I arched my back, flipped over backward, and came down funny. My right hand snapped back in a weird way and I smashed down on my tummy. The strange thing was . . .

my right hand was bent backward and sticking up toward the ceiling!

The basement was silent. I looked up and Marcellus was frozen. He stood over me with his hands on his mouth. I couldn't feel anything in my right arm, and then all of a sudden it felt like a hippo was sitting on my wrist. It felt hot and I couldn't move it. It was the most pain I had ever felt. I couldn't even scream. I tried, but nothing came out. Tears ran down my face so fast, it felt like they had track shoes on.

"Ladybug . . . ladybug . . . are you okay?" Marcellus finally spoke up. I twisted my head around, looked up at him, and finally my voice came back to me.

"MA!!! DADDY!!!" I cried, and wished that the big hippo would get off my wrist.

✿⭐✿⭐5✿⭐✿⭐
Cute Candy-Cane Cast

Ma heard me screaming in the basement and ran down as fast as she could. After seeing my hand bent back, she put a bunch of ice in an ice bag and then held it on my wrist. Ma called Daddy at The Booker Box. He and Ro came home right away. Daddy picked me up just like he did when I was a little baby and carried me to the van. Ma and the boys were already inside. We all rushed to the Bellow Rock Regional Hospital.

When we got to the hospital, Daddy scolded Marcellus. "Boy, what were you thinking? I'll tell you — nothing." Ma and I were waiting in a special emergency room. Ro and Ty went to the restroom and to grab a snack.

"My hand and wrist are hurting *so, so* bad. Can you help me?" I asked the nurse. It felt like that hippo was still squatting on my wrist. Then suddenly more tears came out, and I couldn't stop crying.

The nurse said, "I'm going to try my best, young lady. I think I have just the thing to help you feel better." The nurse was so nice, and he smelled good, too. He gave me a peach lollipop and some medicine to take away the hurt in my hand and wrist. It worked fast, because I didn't hurt too much after that. Then the nurse took an X-ray of my hand and wrist and left to go get the X-ray pictures.

Ma always knows how to make me feel good. I sat on her lap and she stroked my hair and sang in my ear.

"Ruby's all right, she's okay.
She's beautiful
and in her own way.
She's strong,
she's so strong,
and she's my baby."

We were waiting for Ty and Ro to come back. Daddy finished fussing at Marcellus and they left to get a snack. Then the nurse came in my room with the X-ray pictures of my hand and wrist. I was worried about getting in trouble for doing something so crazy.

"Ma, are you and Daddy mad at me for trying to do flips and causing so much trouble?" I asked.

"No, baby, I'm not mad. I was scared when I heard you scream, but not mad," Ma said gently. The soft way Ma spoke made me feel good. "I know you were excited and inspired by what you saw your cousin Keeva doing, but she's seven years older than you. She's had tons of practice. That's why she's so good at flips," Ma explained.

"I just thought that maybe if I tried some of the flips on my own, with the help of Marcellus, I could be as good. Then I could start my own drill team. It didn't turn out so good, huh, Ma?"

"That's okay, Ruby. *You* have to be more careful, and Marcellus has to start using better judgment," Ma said.

"May I come in?" a sweet voice said on the other side of the door.

"Sure. Come on in," I called out. The door opened and in walked a

doctor. She was wearing a long white coat. She had smooth chocolate skin, curly braids, and gold hoop earrings like Ma wears sometimes. She was the prettiest doctor I've ever seen. "My name is Dr. Wells," she said as she shook my left hand.

Daddy and Marcellus walked in

behind Dr. Wells. Marcellus took a seat next to the door. Daddy stood next to me. Marcellus's head was down and it looked like he had been crying. I started to feel sorry for him. I knew he didn't really mean to hurt me. I hoped that maybe he didn't get in too much trouble.

Daddy kissed me on my forehead.

Dr. Wells had my X-rays in her hand. She pinned them up against what looked like a lamp picture frame on the wall. She flicked a switch and the X-rays lit up. I'd never seen a real, live X-ray before. My bone picture looked weird, like a Halloween skeleton arm.

"Wow, I can see every bone in my hand and wrist! That's cool, Dr. Wells!" I was so shocked by what I saw.

"It *is* cool, Ruby. Seems like you have a tiny fracture in your wrist," Dr. Wells said.

"What's a *frack-cher*? Is that bad or good?"

"That means that it's broken. That's the bad news," Dr. Wells explained. "But the good news is that the break is tiny."

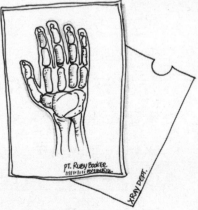

I couldn't tell anything by looking at the X-ray. I guess

doctor eyes are good at seeing things like that.

"So, how do we fix the *frack-cher*, Doc?" I asked.

"What I'm going to have to do is put your right hand and wrist in a cast, Ruby," Dr. Wells explained.

"My right hand? That's my writing hand. My typing-on-my-laptop hand. My scratching hand. My picking-up-things hand. What am I going to do without my good hand, Dr. Wells?"

"Because of the fracture, you'll need a cast so that your little bone can get back to normal. Don't worry. It'll only be on for five to seven weeks," Dr. Wells said.

Ro and Ty had just come into the room. Both of them were holding a bag of corn chips. "Five to seven weeks!" Ro said.

"Come on in and have a seat, boys," Daddy ordered. They sat down at the same time the nurse came in with red, purple, and pink bandages.

Dr. Wells asked, "So, Ruby, what color do you want your cast to be?"

"Would it be any trouble to use purple and red and to make it look like a candy cane? You know, striped?" I really hoped Dr. Wells would say yes.

"No problem, Ruby. I've never done that before, but I can try." She and the nurse began to work right away. They carefully wrapped my candy-cane cast. It didn't take as long as I thought.

By the time they were finished, my right arm looked like a mummy's arm. A *cute* mummy's arm. It was hard and it was stuck in an L shape.

"I like it, Rube. It does look like a giant candy cane," Ty said with a grin.

"Yeah, squirt, you better be careful at school on Monday. Some kid may mistake your arm for the real thing and take a bite!" Ro joked.

Marcellus didn't say a word the whole time. He had a really sad look on his face, and so did I. I started to think how having a cast would stop me from doing a lot of things, especially at school. And maybe the other kids would look at me funny. Most of all, I thought about how long it was going to be before I could put my drill team together. Ma could see the sadness on my face.

She whispered to me. "I love your cast, too, Ruby. Besides, it'll be off before you know it. Things may end up being better than you think."

When Dr. Wells finished with my cast, we all left the room. Marcellus had his head down. "Marcellus, it's okay. Really it is." I tugged on his arm with my good hand.

"I'm just so sorry, ladybug. I'm supposed to protect you and keep you from getting hurt," he said, moping. "I didn't do a good job, did I?"

I wrapped my good arm around Marcellus's waist and then gave him a little hug. "I know you were just trying to help. I'm not mad at you."

Marcellus hugged me back and said, "You're not mad? Good."

I told Marcellus, "I can handle the cast." I raised my arm up as high as I could (which wasn't that high). "It's really Ruby-licious. Everybody at school will love it, don't you think?"

"They sure will. Let's go home, ladybug." He grabbed my good hand and we walked out of the hospital together.

✿ ★ ✿ ★ 6 ✿ ★ ✿ ★
Sweet, Sweet Attention

The next morning my hand and wrist felt a whole lot better. From the time I walked out of the house and onto Chill Brook Avenue, everyone was staring at my candy-cane cast. Kids yelled from their school buses, "NICE CAST, RUBY!" or "SWEET CANDY-CANE ARM, RUBY BOOKER!" I smiled all the way to Hope Road Academy. The day was starting off better than I could have expected.

* * *

"Ruby, what an awesome arm thing!" Manny Flemon said.

"It looks hard. Can I touch it?" whispered Low-Low. His real name is Lionel, but because he speaks so softly, everybody calls him Low-Low.

Since Low-Low talks quietly, I answered him the same way: "Go ahead, Low-Low." He touched my cast carefully. Then Chyna Wentworth touched it. And then almost everybody in Pluto-3, my classroom, rubbed it. I didn't mind that much.

"It sure does look like it hurts, girlie. Are you okay?" asked Teresa.

"I'm okay, girl. It hurt a lot worse yesterday. I'm fine now," I said. "The

only problem I'll have is getting used to doing everything with my left hand. That's all. No biggie."

Everyone crowded around to listen to me. "I was just doing some big-time training, you know — flips and stuff. Teresa and I are starting our own drill team." Everybody thought it was a great idea to put the Chill Brook Steppers together. Everyone except for Marquetta Loopy.

We just don't get along, Marquetta Loopy and I. She thinks that I think that I'm full of myself because I'm the little sister of the Booker boys. Plus, she hates the fact that Miss Fuqua always chooses me to run errands for the class.

Marquetta sat at her desk and didn't even look my way. She was jealous of all the attention I was getting.

When Miss Fuqua stepped out in the hallway to talk to Miss Honeygrove, the second-grade teacher from across the hall, Marquetta came close to my desk to sharpen a pencil. She looked down at me and said, "Nice cast . . . *Ruby Booger.*" She turned up her nose and then trotted back to her desk. She always calls me that when Miss Fuqua isn't listening.

I got up from my seat, even though

Miss Fuqua doesn't want us to do that when she steps out of the room. I stopped Marquetta before she sat down and asked, "What did you just call me?" I cracked my knuckles, the knuckles that weren't in a cast. I was sick of that girl.

Marquetta Loopy saw that I meant business. She caught a big lump in her throat and then said, "Who, me? I didn't say anything, Ruby." I knew she wasn't telling me the whole truth. Finally, she admitted, "I just said, 'nice cast.'"

"That better be all you said. I'm sick of being nice to you. Why do you have

an attitude with me all the time?" I put
my hand on my hip.

"I don't know what you're talking
about," Marquetta said. She was still
not telling the whole truth.

"Yeah, whatever. One day you're
really going to make me angry, girl . . .
watch yourself," I said, steaming. Then

I marched to my seat before Miss Fuqua came back.

"Wow, Ruby, I've never seen you that mad before. That mean Loopy girl sure had it coming, though," Teresa said softly in her usual Tennessee twang.

I wasn't going to let Marquetta get me down. I had a cute cast and an even cuter matching outfit, and everybody else but Marquetta thought so.

As the day went on, things got a little out of hand. I told all of the kids in my class how I hurt myself. But by the time that story got around the school, it came back to me in a dozen different ways. Some of the things I heard were crazy! I just knew the wild stories had "Ro" written all over them.

*   *   *

At lunchtime, a kid named Chester Pootin, a fifth-grader, came up to me and said, "That was very brave of you, Ruby Booker, to run out in the street to save that entire litter of kittens from being run over. I didn't know you had it in you." Chester patted me on the back and chuckled like he was so proud of me. I didn't know what he was talking about.

On the way to the computer lab, a second-grader named Prissy Preston came up to me and held her hand up like she wanted to give me a high five. I gave her one. I didn't know what it was for but I figured there's nothing wrong with giving away high fives every now and then.

She smiled real big and said, "Ruby, I think you're the coolest girl ever, seeing how you went out there and played football with your big brothers and their friends." Then Prissy clapped for me. "I even heard that you hurt yourself when you caught the winning touchdown pass. That's what I'm talking about, girl. Represent!"

And in gym, some kid I didn't even know came up to me with teary eyes and a goofy-looking grin and said, "You're my new hero, Ruby Booker. I heard that you busted into a burning animal hospital, saved a whole floor full of gerbils, and then leaped to safety out a window. Wow, you're amazing." He shook my hand like I was Oprah. Then he just walked away. Things were getting weird.

This was the type of attention I couldn't have seen coming. It wasn't what I thought would happen, but it did make for a strange day. On an errand for Miss Fuqua, I found out with my own eyes and ears who was spreading all of the nutty tales. It was just as I'd guessed.

I had to take a note to one of the third-grade teachers down the hall from our classroom. When I passed the library, I saw a table of five boys. They were all huddled up and listening to one of the boys telling them a secret. At least it looked like a secret.

I had to quietly sneak in the library door. Then I crawled underneath the table next to the boys. They had no idea I was there. I could hear everything the one boy was sharing with the rest of the group. I heard him say in a whispery tone, "Then Ruby jumped off the horse to catch the purse snatcher! We couldn't believe it. My little sister has a lot of guts."

The rest of the group was impressed as they listened to the boy. It was Ro! They were paying close attention to his wild story about me. He had been the one telling the *so* not true stories about me all day. It was too funny. And also not funny. Ro had been like Marquetta, not telling the whole truth. Actually, he wasn't even telling half the truth! Still, I had to put my hand over my mouth so that I wouldn't bust out laughing.

I crawled back out of the library without even being seen. Even though Ro's stories made me laugh, I was disappointed in him. I knew what the truth was.

I was just upset that he never mentioned my drill team to anyone. I guess he doesn't believe I could be a superstar like Kee-Kee, either. That's okay. I was going to prove to him, Marquetta Loopy, and the girls who came to my tryout how fabulous the Chill Brook Steppers could be.

After school, Ma was going to take me to a real, live practice of my cousin Kee-Kee and the Wallace Park Spirit. I would then see how stepping was really done right.

I couldn't wait!

7

Nothing to Do with Flips

Ma was taking me all the way to Wallace Park. It would have been nice to see my friend Mona Sweetroll, but Mona was out of town visiting her grandparents.

I leaned forward from my seat in the back of the van. "How long is this drive, Ma? Seems like we've been riding forever."

"Cool your jets, little lady," Ma said.

"I want to take as many notes as possible for my drill team," I said.

"I have to find out how Kee-Kee's group got so good and how I can get everyone to go bananas for *my* squad."

"What about learning how to actually flip, tumble, and cheer the way the Wallace Park Spirit does so well?"

"Ma, it wasn't just the flipping, the tumbling, and the cheering. The Wallace Park Spirit had something electric that I *felt* when I watched them." I was trying to make Ma see what it really took to be an all-star drill team captain. "It's the style and grace they have. Besides, I can learn all of that other stuff when my wrist gets better."

"Okay, baby," Ma said. "Whatever you say. Just don't get in the way over there, and keep an open mind." We pulled up to the place where the practice was held, the 138th Street Baptist Church. Kee-Kee and her parents belong to that church.

"What do you mean by keeping an open mind?" I asked Ma.

"That means don't be disappointed if you don't see what you came to see. Okay?"

"I guess so, Ma," I answered. I knew I wasn't going to be disappointed, though. "Kee-Kee will amaze me again and teach me how to be just like her. Besides, Ma, can you imagine how gorgeous their practice outfits must be?"

Ma just shook her head like *she* was disappointed in *me*. "Come on, girl. Let's go inside."

* * *

As soon as Kee-Kee saw me, she ran over and gave me and Ma a hug. "Ruby, that's a pretty cast you're wearing. I love it!"

"Thanks, Kee-Kee. Am I on time for practice?"

"You're on time, but we're not really

having our usual practice today," Kee-Kee told me and Ma.

"Why not, Keeva?" Ma asked. "Not enough members to practice?"

"Two days a week, we do something nice for the neighborhood, for the whole Wallace Park area," Kee-Kee told Ma.

I couldn't help but ask, "Is it an

extra-special squad show that you only do for them? And where is your cute practice outfit, girl?" I just had to know. Kee-Kee was wearing a regular-looking purple jumpsuit. It was cute but not what I expected.

"Come with me. I'll show you what we do. As far as my outfit goes, we're not dressed to flip all of the time. What were you thinking?" She laughed a little. Then she led the way over to the church gym.

When we got there, I saw the squad members who had performed the week before. None of them had a shiny, sparkly outfit on. No one was dancing, stepping, or flipping. There was no music. And there was a bunch of people I'd never seen before. It was weird.

"What's going on here, Kee-Kee? Where's the music? And who are all of these people?" This was not the practice I had imagined.

"On Tuesdays we open up the church and feed the homeless or families that may need a helping hand." Kee-Kee pointed at all of the food lined up on the tables. Each and every member of the Wallace Park Spirit wore aprons, loaded up plates, and handed them out to anyone who came in and needed a hot meal. I couldn't believe my eyes.

"Keeva, who set all of this up? You kids?" Ma asked. She seemed so impressed by what she saw. I wasn't. This had nothing to do with drill team stuff.

"I kinda did, Aunt Fatima," Kee-Kee said to Ma. "Most of the kids in the squad go to my school. They were all glad to do it."

"What do you guys do on the other days?" Ma was really into what Kee-Kee and her friends had going. It was no big deal to me.

"On Thursdays we have elementary school kids here for tutoring sessions. We show them how to do math, science, and reading. Just regular school stuff," Kee-Kee explained as she handed a cup of punch to a little boy about my size. There were grown-ups in old clothes. I saw whole families that looked tired but so happy just to be there.

"I am so, so proud of you, darling," Ma said, praising Kee-Kee. Then she gave her a gigantic hug and kissed her on the cheek. "I know your mother is even prouder than I am."

"Excuse me, Ma." I threw Ma a big fake smile, grabbed Kee-Kee by the arm, and pulled her to the side. "What is all of this? How can I be like you if I don't see you practicing in your cute squad outfits or see any of your amazing routines? How am I going to start my own drill team? Let's get to it, girl!" I whispered with tight lips. And, oh, was I serious.

"Ruby, you need to check yourself. Honestly." Kee-Kee jerked her arm away from me. She is a teenager and a lot bigger than I am. "What we do as a drill team is much more than what you saw in our show."

"I thought that all you did was make crowds go crazy, lead parades, and sign autographs for all of Wallace Park." I was confused.

Kee-Kee looked at me and shook her head. Then she pointed to a sign on the wall in the gym and asked me, "What does that say up there?"

"It says 'The Home of the Wallace Park Spirit — the Number One Drill Team.'" I read really loud so that I could hear my voice echo in the gym.

"Do you know what that means?" Kee-Kee asked. It was one of those questions that you don't really answer. "Listen, Ruby. You thought all we did was look cute, do super-double-whammy flips, and make pyramids, right?"

"No, I just . . . well, yeah, I did." I couldn't tell a lie.

"That sign says that we represent where we live. If we're going to use the name of the neighborhood we love so much, that means we have to give back to it. It's called community service."

"We do that sometimes," I told her. And that was the truth. "Ma takes us down to shelters and we give them our old toys, clothes, and canned foods."

"Doesn't it make you feel good when you do that?" Kee-Kee asked.

I nodded. "When I help people, everybody feels good. Daddy says the things we pass along will make others happy, and I like that."

"The dancing, flipping, and the tumbling are fun, and we work hard at it," Kee-Kee explained. "But our neighborhood has given so much to every member of the Spirit. So we're kind of like cheerleaders for Wallace Park and the people who live here. We love Wallace Park. It's the least we can do two days a week to help the neighborhood."

"I know what you mean. I love Chill Brook Avenue, too." I started to feel what Kee-Kee was talking about. "But I can't flip or dance or do any of that cool stuff that you do."

Kee-Kee put her arms around me and said, "Don't worry about all of that, little cousin. Performing will come to you. You're a natural, especially the way you sing." That made me feel good. Then she asked, "What's the name of the squad you're starting up?"

"We're the Chill Brook Steppers.

Don't you just love that name?" I knew she would.

"I sure do. And don't you think everyone who lives on Chill Brook Avenue would be proud that you were representing them?" she asked.

"I sure do!"

"Well, give them something to be proud of and give your Steppers something to stand for. The cute outfits and cool routines will come together. Trust me, cousin." Kee-Kee latched me by the arm and walked me back over to Ma. Then she joined the rest of her squad to help pass out the food.

I called out to her, "Kee-Kee, aren't you going to sign my candy cane?" Up until that point, I only had a few inky names scribbled on my cast.

"Yeah . . . maybe I will later," she answered. Without even looking over at me, she joined her team to help with the food. I thought that Kee-Kee didn't want to sign my cast because she was too busy thinking about feeding the homeless.

Ma asked, "So, what were you girls talking about?"

"Just talking about outfits, flips, and how to really become a neighborhood superstar."

✿⭒✿⭒8✿⭒✿⭒
Let Me Get That for You

Sometimes when I get out of school, I like to take Lady Love for a walk along Chill Brook Avenue. The next day I put on her little pink fake diamond leash and we walked like two divas. We looked so cool together.

I only walk up to the stoplight on Fifty-fifth Street and then turn around. Ma won't let me go too far by myself. As we walked, I could hear her call out, "All right, little Miss Booker and little green diva, Mama misses you. Come back." Whenever we go for a walk, Ma keeps an eye on us. Today she was on the stoop reading a fashion magazine.

On my way down the street, I thought about everything Kee-Kee had told me. I thought about all the things her squad does for Wallace Park. I had no idea how I was going to come close to being like her and the Wallace Park Spirit. I was starting to think about just forgetting the whole thing. Maybe I'd stick to singing and being the third-grade Trivia Queen. Maybe that was good enough.

But when I got three houses away from our house, I saw something that changed my mind quickly.

Our neighbor, sweet Mrs. Vine, was slowly coming toward me and Lady Love, pulling a heavy-looking cart on wheels. I don't know how old Mrs. Vine is, but it's probably as much as Ma and Daddy put together.

"Hey, sugar. How's school going?" Mrs. Vine asked. She looked really tired, and the sacks in her cart looked so full.

"School is a piece of cake, Mrs. V. Third grade is so much fun," I told her as I fed Lady Love a piece of banana.

"I remember when I was in the third grade. That was ages ago, sugar."

Mrs. Vine was hunched over a little and breathing kind of heavy. I couldn't let her pull that cart any farther. She lived two more houses down. "Can I help you, Mrs. V?"

"Oh, well, *sure*, sugar." She gave me the cart handle. The cart was kind of heavy, but it wasn't too heavy for me to pull.

"Are you just coming from the Fifty-seventh Street Market, Mrs. V? Looks like you've got a lot of stuff." I pulled the cart with my good hand. Lady Love walked next to us.

Ma saw what I was doing and yelled out, "Hi, Mrs. Vine. Ruby's helping you out, huh?"

Mrs. Vine turned to Ma and said as

loud as she could, "Yes, she is. You should be proud to have such a sweet little girl. She's just as sweet as she can be." My cheeks got warm and I could feel them turning red. That happens when people say super-nice things about me.

"So how often do you have to go to the store, Mrs. V?" I wanted to know. An idea was starting to stir up in my brain.

"Mostly I go on Wednesdays. It just depends on how I'm feeling. Sometimes I'm too tired to even walk to my front door." When Mrs. Vine said that, it made me think.

"So do you always go to the store alone?" Ideas were still coming to me.

"Most of the time I go with Mr. Brumley across the way, or Miss Pepperburg next door. There's a whole lot of us old-timers who walk together to get groceries." I knew all of the old people Mrs. Vine named. They have all lived in this neighborhood for a long time.

When Mrs. Vine and I made it to her house, she tried to lift one of the bags out of her cart.

"Don't worry about it, Mrs. V. You go and open the door and I'll bring the bags up," I offered.

"Are you sure, sugar?" she looked back at me and asked.

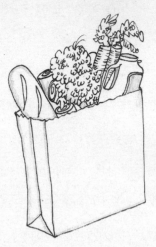

"Yes, I'm sure. No problem." I gladly picked up one sack at a time and took it inside. I did it with only one hand. It felt good to help.

After I was done, Mrs. V tried to offer me money for helping her. I just couldn't take it. "No, thank you, Mrs. V. I would do this anytime for you," I told her.

Once, Daddy told me and my brothers, "Don't ever do a good deed for someone because you expect something in return." That means you should do stuff because you're being nice, not for money or anything. It was like Daddy was standing there telling me this, and I heard him loud and crystal clear.

After I pulled Mrs. V's grocery cart up the stairs, too, I picked up Lady Love and scrammed back to my house. "Bye, Mrs. V. I've got some Chill Brook Steppers work to do."

"Bye, sugar. And thank you again," she hollered out from her front window.

She seemed happier, sitting up in that window, smiling. I wondered if I'd had something to do with that.

"Slow down, baby. Where are you going?" Ma asked. I rocketed up our stoop and headed inside.

"I'm about to bring more smiles to Chill Brook Avenue. You'll see!"

9

Something to Be Proud Of

Two days after I helped Mrs. V with her groceries, I held another meeting with Teresa, the Piccolo twins, and Toya Tribbles. They didn't look too interested in what I had to say, not even my girl Teresa. "Ladies, here we are again. And this time around, things are going to be a little different."

Teresa twisted a piece of bubble gum in her mouth. "Okay, girlie, I know we can't be here learning any moves. You've still got some ways to go with that cast on your little wrist." She had on the most stylish pair of cowgirl boots I've ever seen. But style wasn't why I called the Chill Brook Steppers all together.

"Yeah, Booker. Don't waste my time again," Toya said with her arms folded tight. She rolled her eyes *and* neck at me. "Got any new bright ideas besides how cute we're going to look?"

"I sure . . ." Peaches began to say.

". . . hope so, Ruby Booker." As usual, her twin, Plenty, finished the sentence. They were wearing matching roller skates. They looked cute, too. But it wasn't why we were meeting.

"I've thought about it, and if we're going to be the Chill Brook Steppers, we've got to represent." I walked back and forth in front of the girls.

"So you still don't know how to dance or do drill team steps?" Toya wanted to know.

"Nope," I answered with a grin.

"And you still can't..." started Peaches.

"...do a backflip?" finished Plenty.

"Not with this on." I held my cast as high as I could.

Teresa whispered to me, "Uh, Ruby, you got anything else up your little candy-cane cast?"

"Well, remember when I told you guys that I went to see my cousin's drill team perform, and how crazy the crowd was for them?" I asked.

"Yeah . . ." they all said together.

"Now I know why that crowd went bonkers for the Wallace Park Spirit. It had nothing to do with what they had on or how high they jumped," I continued.

"What was it, the loud music?" Toya joked. She sure does have a smarty-pants mouth sometimes.

"No, Toya. Those people cheered their hearts out because they really love the kids who make up the Wallace

Park Spirit. They're proud of where they live and they show it on and off the stage," I explained.

The girls looked puzzled. "So what are we gonna do?" Teresa asked.

"We're going to be a drill team that Chill Brook Avenue can be proud of. We're going to do good things, too." I walked over to my guitar-shaped book bag and pulled out five purple T-shirts with our names on the front and THE CHILL BROOK STEPPERS on the back. I also had lists of names and houses where older people like Mrs. Vine lived.

"Nice T-shirts, but what happened to the fancy outfit you had on the last time

we got together?"
Toya asked me.

"I put it away
for now. I think
that first we need
to prove that we
are worthy enough
to have *Chill Brook* in our name," I told
the girls. Then I gave them the lists of
names.

"What are we..." said Plenty
this time.

"...gonna do with these?" Peaches
capped off the question.

"We're going to be there for all of
the older people who live on Chill
Brook. If they need us to help them

with groceries, we do it. If they need their stoop swept, we do it. If they want us to walk their pets, we get it done," I said, breaking it down to my squad mates.

"I get it! The more nice things we do, the more everybody on Chill Brook will see that we are something good for our neighborhood, right?" Teresa started to see where I was coming from.

"That's it, T. That's it. Something good and fabulous." I gave her a high five.

"Sounds great to me, Booker. But what about our shows?" Toya asked.

"When are we going to become the kind of drill team that actually does steps, moves, and backflips?"

"I don't know, Toya. Maybe when my cast is off, we can start practicing." I spoke to Toya the way Kee-Kee would to her squad members. "We'll get to that soon. Let's make a name for ourselves first."

"Sounds good . . ." Peaches blurted as she and her sister spun around in a circle on their skates.

". . . to us! Let's do it, Steppers!" Plenty cheered.

We all got into a circle, slid our purple T-shirts on, put our hands in the center, and I said, "On three, give me a loud and proud Chill Brook Steppers cheer! *One...two... three!*"

"CHILL BROOK STEPPERS!!!" all five of us roared to the sky.

❀★❀★10❀★❀★
You Know You're Big When . . .

A few weeks later, Ma was in the den, sewing a pretty new dress for one of her friends. The doorbell rang. "Get the door, somebody!" Ma yelled out.

"I got it!" I yelled back. I was in the kitchen making a snack. You just can't beat grape Jell-O and fruit cocktail.

When I made it to our front door, I saw a tall girl standing outside. It was Kee-Kee! I ran to open the door, and when I looked out behind her, I almost fainted.

"Yes, does Ruby Booker, the captain of the Chill Brook Steppers, live here?" Kee-Kee asked in a funny voice. Every single member of the Wallace Park Spirit was with her. Each and every one. I think I counted lots of big kids. They had their drums and pom-poms. Plus, they were all wearing their red-white-and-gold performance outfits. Kee-Kee had her hair done like a girl in a magazine ad. She was looking extra-extra pretty.

"Where are all of you headed?" I asked, still in shock.

"Your mother told us about you finally starting your squad and about all of the nice things you guys are planning. I love it, Ruby!" She hugged me and lifted me off the ground.

"Are you going to a competition?" I wondered.

"Nope. We just decided to come over here before practice and ask if we could possibly . . . all of us . . . sign your cast." Kee-Kee said it like she thought I was a neighborhood superstar.

"Can you sign my cast? Sure!" I ran and got pens of all colors. The Wallace Park Spirit stood in line and signed my cast one at a time. It was like a dream come true.

They all signed, stood in the middle

of the street, played their music, and marched down Chill Brook Avenue.

"See you later, cousin!" Kee-Kee waved her baton in the air. And just like that, they were gone.

Tyner came to the door and said, "Who was that, Rube? Sounded like a herd of elephants marching."

"Not really a herd, Ty. It was more like the second-best drill team in the world, that's all."

"Second-best? Well, who's the first?" Ty scratched his head and looked confused.

I turned around to show him what my purple T-shirt said on the back.

Then, as I walked away with a little wiggle, I said, "Ty . . . do you really have to ask? I mean, really?"

One minute, you feel like it's all about you. But really — it's not. There are things a lot more important than being cute, getting a lot of attention, and having a fan club. Maybe being helpful and caring about people are ways to make a better you . . . isn't that what matters most? A sweeter, nicer, more helpful Ruby Booker. I think so.

— rb

⭐ Ruby Booker's Out-of-the-Blue Nice Stuff to Do ⭐

- Say hi to a kid at your school whom you've never spoken to before.
- Sit next to someone at lunch who sits by him- or herself most of the time.
- Tell your mom how pretty she looks today.
- Give your dessert away to someone.
- Be the one to say you're sorry first.
- Help your grandparents clean the house.

- Bake something with your mom.
- Tell your dad or the father figure in your life how much he means to you.
- Have a yard sale, bake sale, or lemonade sale, and give the money you earn to a charity or a family in need. Ask a grown-up to help.
- Help an elderly or disabled neighbor with his or her yard by gardening, mowing the lawn, shoveling snow, or raking leaves.
- Volunteer at a children's hospital and spend some time with another kid whom you don't know. Play

board and video games, talk, or just hang out.

- Get together with other kids in your neighborhood and pick up the litter on your block.

Collect them all!

Look out, world, here comes Ruby Marigold Booker!

Ultra-fabulous Ruby Booker has what it takes to step out of the shadows of her older brothers. She's smart and full of great ideas for filling the spotlight. Ruby knows what she wants and goes for it—even if going for it sometimes means going way out on a limb (or breaking a limb, perhaps) to show the world that she means business. But when the going gets tough, thank goodness Ruby can call on her best friend, Teresa, her pet iguana, Lady Love, and a family who's by her side, no matter what. Read all the Ruby books and have fun with Bellow Rock's newest star!

New York Times **Bestselling Author**

Sharon M. Draper

Sassy

Little Sister Is NOT My Name!

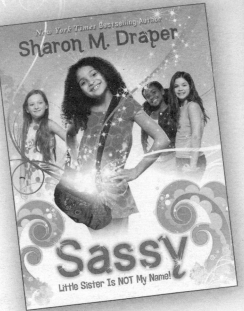

It's not easy being nine, especially when you're Sassy Simone Sanford and you've been named for sticking out your tongue on the day you were born. Especially when you're the youngest in the family and everyone drives you crazy by calling you Little Sister.

But nothing stops Sassy's imagination and style. With the help of her friends Jasmine, Carmelita, Holly, and Travis, life is a sparkling adventure. But when trouble comes, all Sassy has to do is reach into her shimmery Sassy Sack to find just what's needed—a camera, shoestring, flashlight, or super-glue—and problems get solved fast.

Sister Magic

BY ANNE MAZER

Sibling Rivalry with a Magical Twist!

"A humorous chapter book, easy to read and full of fun."
—*Children's Literature*

High-flying Ruby
soars to new heights!

I'm Ruby Booker, and I mean business. The plan is simple: My BFF, Teresa Petticoat, and I are going to be the best flipping, dancing drill team in Bellow Rock! All we have to do is learn some moves. That's where my big brother Marcellus comes in. Even though he's not a cheerleader, he's super-fun and I'm sup[...]teach me how to flip. Then I can teach Teresa. And who knows? Maybe this cheerleading thing will land us in the spotlight at Chill Brook Elementary!

★ ★ ★ ★ ★

"Ruby is cooler than cool!" –Dobbin, age 8

SCHOLASTIC
www.scholastic.com

Cover art by Vanessa Brantley Newton
Cover design by Alison Klapthor

$4.99 US / $6.50 CAN
RL3 002–005

ISBN-13: 978-0-545-01763-3
ISBN-10: 0-545-01763-7

50499

9 780545 017633

LITTLE
APPLE

S